ATHLiTACOMiCS™
DESIGN TEAM:

Writer and Creator – **Israel Idonije**

Illustration – **Renzo RF**

Creative Direction – **Ron Marz & Bart Sears**

SPECIAL THANKS TO:

Emmanuel Idonije,
Teresa Myers, Kelley Speck,
Janell Nelson and Joe "Cujodah" Nelson

Teach Love.

A portion of every book purchase will support iF Charities and its mission to impact communities by providing programs focused on social and emotional life skills.

#TeachLove

Post your DreamKidz pictures with #TeachLove for a chance to win special prizes!

This book is dedicated to young
girls and boys all over the world
who will grow to make
our world a more loving place.
Give yourself a big hug!

I LOVE YOU.

I LOVE ME!

A special kid, with lots of gifts,
for all the world to see.

From head to toe, my light will glow,
bright and beautifully.

I Love my eyes!

They help me see the
butterflies and bumblebees.

I Love my nose!

It helps me breathe the fresh,
clean air and summer breeze.

I Love my **hands!**

My fingers hold the hands
of those I love the most.

I Love my mouth!

I shout and say:
I'm thankful for another day!

I Love my ears!

They help me hear my friends talking,
far and near.

I Love my legs, feet and knees!

They help me run,
and jump with glee.

Every part made perfectly!

I Love myself!

I LOVE ME!

I LOVE ME!

Thanks for reading!

WHAT DO YOU LOVE?

Tell us on the next page!

I ❤ LOVE ...

Write down some things YOU love!

Follow The DreamKidz Adventures

Instagram: @DreamKidzAdventures

Follow ATHLiTACOMiCS

Facebook: ATHLiTACOMiCS

Twitter: @ATHLiTACOMiCS